KYLA MA

miss.behaves

around the world

written & illustrated by

kyla may

PSS!
PRICE STERN SLOAN

Copyright © 2005 by Kyla May Pty Ltd. All rights reserved. Published by Price Stern Sloan, a division of Penguin Young Readers Group, 345 Hudson Street, New York, New York 10014. PSS! is a registered trademark of Penguin Group (USA) Inc. Printed in China.

Library of Congress Cataloging-in-Publication Data

May, Kyla.
Kyla May Miss. Behaves : around the world / by Kyla May.
  p. cm.
Summary: During geography class, Kyla May writes in her journal about daydreams that carry her and her French poodle, Fifi-belle, to Paris, Japan, and other exotic locations far from the Melbourne, Australia, creative arts school she attends.
 ISBN 0-8431-1371-5 (pbk.) — ISBN 0-8431-1458-4 (hardcover)
 (1. Imagination—Fiction. 2. Voyages and travels—Fiction. 3. Geography—Fiction. 4. Schools—Fiction. 5. Diaries—Fiction. 6. Australia—Fiction.) I. Title: Kyla May Miss Behaves : around the world. II. Title: Kyla May misbehaves : around the world. III. Title.

PZ7.M4535Ky 2005
(Fic)—dc22

2004021347

ISBN 978-0-8431-1371-6 (pbk.)   10 9 8
ISBN 0-8431-1458-4 (hc)   10 9 8 7 6 5 4 3 2 1

G'DAY, MY NAME'S KYLA MAY. (in case you've forgotten! ☺) i'm the girl from Australia with the WiLD imagination.

But i promise i'm trying real hard 2 concentrate in class & i reckon my JOURNALS R sure helping the cause — like, i'm not getting in TROUBLE half as much, well...mayB a third?!

Anyways, WELCOME back 2 the continuing ADVENTURES of MY life. But hey, don't expect much, since it's GEOGRAPHY class @ this precise moment in time...(Zzzzz zzz zzz...oops, i almost fell asleep). Swear 2 U, GEOGRAPHY's the boringest class ever. ☹

very active imagination

Zzzzzz

Hello, I am Fifi-belle, Kyla May's gorgeous dog.

this is ME!

C my special dictionary @ back of journal!

btw: This is my absolutely gorgeous doggie: Fifi-belle

3

✿ Here is my GEOGRAPHY class: 🐞

Yeah! Disco Dancing!

This photo was taken on our last field trip — 📷 a 'disco tour' of the Aussie outback. Initially i was totally excited 'cause i thought we were going DISCO DANCING in the bush — (have i ever mentioned how totally fabulous i am on the dance floor?) But ☹ it ended u being a 'discovery tour'! Hmmm...totally disappointing! 🐌

my fave Aussie animals:

1st: koala

2nd: wombat

3rd: kangaroo

This is 'perfect' Bianca Boticelli. Unfortunately Bianca & i don't see eye 2 eye that often. Let's just say, we test each other's patience!

This is **Miki Minski** (my bestest friend in the whole world) & ME (of course!) We dressed up in 'camouflage' so Bianca couldn't find us! (btw: when hiding from your enemy...wear camouflage clothing...enemy in this situation = Bianca! hee hee.) & here's my 2nd bestest friend Sienna Longmore.

On our 'disco tour,' i so tricked **Ms. Biggleton** by
stowing **Fifi-belle**, my absolutely gorgeous **French Poodle**, in my BACKPACK! **Fifi-BELLE** wanted 2
experience the 'outback' 2...& i share EVERYTHING
with **Fifi-belle** — so why not school trips?
U can almost see her in this Photo!!!!!

my teacher

Fifi's 1970s Disco Diva
outfit (Mum says the
1970s were the 'Disco Era'

of course, Miki was in on my secret!

Fifi-BELLE

Disco Diva

6

the French flag

Eiffel Tower:
V.famous landmark
Avenue des Champs-Elysées

Anyhow, in PARIS (that's in **France**) dogs go EVERYWHERE with their owners...

Let's move to France! I'm begging!

❀ 2 work...

❀ 2 restaurants...

PARIS

❀ ...even 2 boutiques!

Dioré
CHANNELE

As we all know, **Fifi-BELLE**'s **French**, there4 she's different from non-**French** dogs, she totally knows how 2 behave. She had an awesome day discovering the **bush** & accompanying ME in some disco moves!!!! (Even though she was hidden, she still wore her **DISCO OUTFIT!**) ☺

Here's my teacher **Ms. Biggleton**. i used 2 call her 'BUG-EYE' & think she was sooooo boring, but now she completely (understands) ME & encourages my creativity thru extra after-school classes, like painting & computer graphics. Even though i stay later, i L♥VE it! But don't 4 a second even *think* i've turned in2 a NERD!............Like, HELLO!!! Hanging out @ school can actually B COOL (& a million, billion, zillion times better than Detention!)

"KYLA MAY, i UNDERSTAND YOU WELL. AS A CHILD i WAS VERY MUCH LIKE YOU. MIGHT i SUGGEST ADDITIONAL CLASSES TO EXPRESS YOUR GIFTED IMAGINATION?"

stranger things have happened!

Nerds are cool!

now, that's more like it!

Kyla May as a Nerd

yeah...right!

advanced chemistry

extra difficult history

almost impossible poetry

really hard math

Kyla May as an Artist

As a result, i'm concentrating loads better in class, oh, except 4 NOW! Oops, it's actually GEOGRAPHY class—s'pose i better listen 2 what Ms. B's saying...stay tuned...

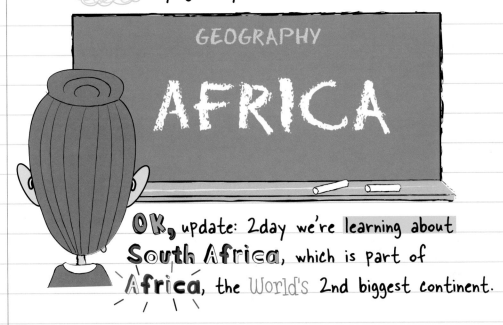

GEOGRAPHY

AFRICA

OK, update: 2day we're learning about South Africa, which is part of Africa, the World's 2nd biggest continent.

Africa's totally amazing 'cause of all the really COOL 'wild animals' roaming the land (sort of similar 2 my classroom!...Hmmm...i think Wally Willyman looks like a monkey!... imagine a bunch of Wallys running around... how funny! hee hee!) i've only ever seen African animals B4 @ the ZOO!

Wally ←→ monkey
oops, i mean the other way round!!!

an African tree

a cheetah

a hippo

a zebra

an elephant

a rhino

I'd love to go on safari! Let's go!

African art

a safari hat

a lion cub

a giraffe

SOUTH AFRICA
COOL FACTS & FIGURES

LOCATION: SOUTHERN TIP OF AFRICA

LANGUAGE: ELEVEN OFFICIAL LANGUAGES INCLUDING AFRIKAANS & ENGLISH

POPULATION: 42,718,530

SIZE: 1,219,912 SQ KM (ALMOST TWICE THE SIZE OF TEXAS)

CAPITAL CITY: PRETORIA

FAVE LANDMARK: TABLE MOUNTAIN

FAVE FOOD: CHICKEN PIRI-PIRI

FAVE ANIMALS: ELEPHANTS & LIONS

MY FAVE CITIES: JOHANNESBURG & CAPE TOWN

FASHION CAPITAL: JOHANNESBURG

FAVE HOBBY: GOING ON SAFARI

MAP:

FLAG:

PRETORIA
JOHANNESBURG
SOUTH AFRICA
TABLE MOUNTAIN
CAPE TOWN

10

Ms. B's brought in photos from her **South African SAFARI** (btw: Safari = a sightseeing trip, usually in a JEEP exploring **Africa**'s wildlife). How **COOL** !! ☺

rhinoceroses may B totally cute, but in fact they're the most dangerous animals ever if U get 'em angry... so **WATCH OUT!** (hmmm...sounds a bit like my Aunt Mavis!) ☹

Hmmm... just imagine ME in a pink Safari suit? ♡♥♡ ...2 cute!

African elephants R the ones with the HUGE ears...whereas Indian elephants have small ones...**actually, speaking of Aunt Mavis — she also has HUGE, no make that MASSIVE ears!**

★ Hmmm....*imagine* going on SAFARI!

☆ ...ohhhh, i could wear the cutest lil' SAFARI outfit ...i can just see it now...Pink, Pink on Pink!

★ Hmmm...Fifi & i could feed the Giraffes...

☆ ...& *hang out* with the Elephants...

⭐ ...run with the Cheetahs, well @ least TRY our very best!...

eeek!!! They're NOT rocks!

⭐ ...& play on, oops i mean WITH the Hippos...

⭐ ...& mayB have fun with the Big Cats! (nice kitty cats) ...hmmm...on 2nd thought...mayB NOT! ★ ★ ★ ☆

☆ Oops... back 2 reality! Nearly got caught daydreaming! PHEW, that was a close 1! OK...CONCENTRATE, KYLA!

☆ Ms. B has assigned a 'CREATIVE' project. (Yeah!...right up my alley!) She's divided us in2 groups of ③ alphabetically.

Yeah!!! x3

Sienna Longmore
Kyla May
Miki Minski

(Unreal! Miki, Sienna & i R together!!!!!!! How COOL that our names follow one another's on the class roll.) ☺ @ the end of the week, a member from each group will present their project 2 the rest of class.

iMAGiNATiON

The project is: (fill in the blank)
IMAGINE YOU ARE FROM ????????????????

We can choose any country in the world & imagine what it'd B like 2 come from there. ....Hey, when it comes 2 using your imagination -like, i've totally got it covered!

14

⭐ Hmmm...

Turkey?
India?
France?
China?
United States?
Imagine i'm from????
Mexico?
England?

No surprise – Bianca's like T☺TALLY jealous of **our group** & "vowed" 2 beat us & TOP the class...as if! No chance! After all...

KYLA MAY = genius @ work.

GENIUS AT WORK

Better go home & start thinking of project ideas!!!
☆ ☆ ☆ ☆ ☆ ☆ ☆

SOMEONE'S NOT HAPPY

Yes, I am the best dog ever!

Can't wait 2 brainstorm with FiFi-BELLE – she's such a good listener. She even wags her tail when she likes my ideas!! Is she the best dog in the WORLD, or what?!

Just told MUM & DAD about my project & they suggested Japan, since we went there last year on holiday. Here R our happy snaps:

Bonsai: famous Japanese plant

This is a Japanese temple - unfortunately Dad mucked up the camera's self-timer!

This is Mount Fuji, Japan's highest mountain.

as usual, Mum likes 2 dress up - this time as Japanese, of course!

Cherry blossoms R famous in Japan & celebrate spring. They're so beautiful but only bloom a couple of days every year. People travel from all over to catch a glimpse of the blossoms.

good-luck cats

i've never EVER seen soooooo many people B4 in my life! The population is more than 6x Australia's!!! (& i complain about hot days when my beach is totally crowded. That's nothing

In Japan funky techno gizmos & space-age buildings R like EVERYWHERE, but there R also loads of traditional houses, temples, food & outfits. It's a total combo of the old & new

16

GOOD

LUCK

JAPAN
COOL FACTS & FIGURES

LOCATION: EASTERN ASIA

LANGUAGE: JAPANESE

POPULATION: 127,333,002

SIZE: 377,835 SQ KM

 (SLIGHTLY LARGER THAN ARIZONA)

CAPITAL CITY: TOKYO

FAVE LANDMARK: MOUNT FUJI – JAPAN'S

HIGHEST MOUNTAIN

FAVE FOOD: SUSHI

FAVE ANIMAL: SNOW MONKEY

MY FAVE CITIES: TOKYO, OSAKA

FASHION CAPITAL: TOKYO

FAVE HOBBY: SUMO WRESTLING

MAP:

FLAG:

JAPAN

MT FUJI ★

OSAKA

TOKYO

sushi: YUM

a Japanese fan

a lantern

Mmmm, I love sushi too. Delicious!

17

But i must tell U the <u>absolute best</u> thing about **Japan** the **toys** & **CARTOONS** — they totally ROCK!

Here R some of my FAVE **toys**, some R NEW & some R older 'traditional' **toys**:

Traditional Toys

My Porcelain Doll

My Kokeshi Wooden Doll

Fifi-belle's Koma
(spinning top)

My Tako
(traditional
Japanese Kite)

New Toys

my pussy-cat wobbler

meeoooow

my mini-robot Dog

2450

GLAMOUR PUSS

my electronic game

my backpack 'weird creature'

Toys i made myself!

an eagle

a whale

a crane

This is **Origami**: paper folding 2 crea[t] animals (no scissors [o] glue needed — oh, but [ ] drew on the eyes!)

Hmmm...imagine ME & Fifi-belle as Japanese cartoon characters...

The Adventures of Sensei Kyla May & Ninja Fifi-belle

i'm a master defender in chopstick martial arts... & Fifi's collar is a fierce fighting weapon

What a sensational Ninja I am!

☺ The streets R safe once more.

19

It's lunchtime: **Miki**, Sienna & i catch up 2 brainstorm. Sienna suggests **Italy** 'cause her grandparents R from a city called PiSa. Hey, apparently there's a building there that's totally falling over!!! It's called the:

★ ☆ ★ **Leaning Tower of Pisa** ★ ☆ ★

✿ BEFORE ✿

Hmmmm...how ridiculous no one's ever thought 2 STRAIGHTEN it!

Like, i'm not a TOTAL control freak, but surely someone should have done this already. Like, HELLO!

Oh no, my group can't make a decision on our project Sienna wants **Italy**, i mentioned **Japan** & Miki's unsure

But i don't *think* either country is IMAGINATIVE enough Ms. B wants us 2 B "creative," there4 we MUST really use our *imagination!* (☹ However, Miki & Sienna say use MY *imagination* 2 MUCH...since it always gets me i trouble! Pleeease! i'm totally going 2 think of the absolute bestest project idea EVER. They'll see!) Hmmm...Hmmm... Oops, sooooo late 4 GEOGRAPHY class, better run..

♡ ♡ ♡ ♡ ♡ ♡ ♡ ♡ ♡ ♡ ♡ ♡ ♡ ♡

BAD NEWS!!!... Ms. B wants each group 2 reveal their country. (eek!! — Miki & Sienna look @ me nervously... What R we going 2 do?????)

Bianca Boticelli leaps up 1st (like of course...SO typical!) She announces **Italy**. (Oh dear... Sienna is V. disappointed.) ☹

"...Italy"

POOR SIENNA ☹ ☹ ☹

Between U & ME (oh, & fifi-belle!) i'm actually a teeny weeny bit relieved Bianca chose **Italy**.

22

The ① thing Miki, Sienna & ♡ i DO AGREE on is originality.
There's no way Sienna will want **Italy** anymore. But she's
still upset. MayB i'll write her a note ~~~~~> ☺
& cheer her up:

Dear Sienna,
i know you are upset about Miss Perfect Bianca
choosing Italy. But don't worry, we will

Eeek!!!

"KYLA MAY! WHAT ARE YOU DOING?
WRITING NOTES IN CLASS?
REMEMBER, LACK OF ATTENTION
EQUALS DETENTION!
NEXT TIME, IT'S STRAIGHT
TO THE PRINCIPAL'S OFFICE!"

(i can breathe again!)

(Ouch!!!! That was 2 close 4 comfort!) **Good news though:**
we're not the ONLY group without a country!
Ms. B wants the undecided students 2 *choose* their countries
(that's us)
by "spinning" the globe of the world. 2 pick a country, we
STOP the globe "spinning" with our fingers. Wherever our fingers
land = our country. (Hmmm...not sure i like this??????
Like, *imagine* if we get a MAJOR booooring
country! Like, hello, i just don't do B☹☹☹RING!) 23

Tara Tiara goes 1st. Her finger lands on the **U.S.**
i go 2 the **U.S.** (*United States of America*) heaps, usually New York.
My fave landmark is 'The Statue of Liberty' — i see it from my hotel window.
Mum said it was a present from **France** 2 *America*.

(Mental note: must ask 4 BIGGER Christmas presents!)

the U.S. flag

(MayB i should give Miki a Statue of Liberty?)

The Statue of Liberty

Kyla May

Fifi-belle   Mum   DAD   Mum

The Statue is almost 120 years old (wow, that's old!) It celebrates "freedom, democracy & international friendship."
Hmmm...surely at THAT age, the Statue could do with a face-lift? Like, my Aunt Saffron has them all the time!!
she's totally weirder than Mum!

Hey, i know the PERFECT new face!

it's where the best-ever hot dogs come from!

U.S.

BEFORE

AFTER

☺

what about MY face!?!

Like, what a total, major IMPROVEMENT!

25

U.S.A.
COOL FACTS & FIGURES

LOCATION: BETWEEN CANADA & MEXICO

LANGUAGE: ENGLISH

FLAG:

POPULATION: 293,027,571

SIZE: 9,631,418 SQ KM

(ABOUT HALF THE SIZE OF RUSSIA)

CAPITAL CITY: WASHINGTON DC

FAVE LANDMARK: THE STATUE OF LIBERTY

FAVE FOOD: HOT DOGS & HAMBURGERS

FAVE ANIMALS: BUFFALO & EAGLES

MY FAVE CITIES: NEW YORK CITY & LOS ANGELES

FASHION CAPITAL: NEW YORK

FAVE HOBBIES: SHOPPING & MOVIES

ALASKA

INCLUDING
THIS TOO

MAP:

UNITED STATES
OF AMERICA

CHICAGO

STATUE
OF LIBERTY

NYC

LA

WASHINGTON DC

HAWAII

MIAMI

Amber Van Wiggle spins the globe next. (Hmmm...i really like her hair clips! Wonder where she got 'em?)

Amber's finger lands on **EGYPT**.

Mmmm...nice!!!

GEOGRAPHY

IMAGINE YOU ARE FROM ___EGYPT___?

We know all about **EGYPT** from **History class**. It's famous 4 its ancient history & art. The Sphinx & the Pyramids R amazing. They were created thousands of years ago — like, the **EGYPTIANS** were SO creative, almost AS creative AS ME!!!! (well, nearly!) Hmmm...mayB i'm Part Egyptian?

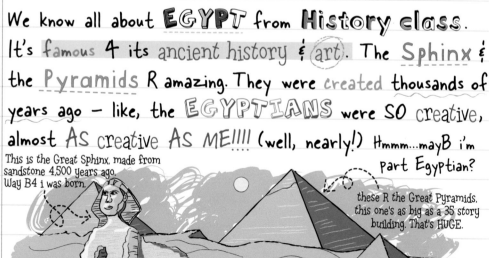

This is the Great Sphinx, made from sandstone 4,500 years ago. Way B4 i was born.

these R the Great Pyramids. this one's as big as a 35 story building. That's HUGE.

Check out how small humans R in comparison. (oh, & camels)

Egyptian icon

Egyptian column

a mummy

I'm a treasure, however NOT ancient!

Egyptian icon

EGYPT
COOL FACTS & FIGURES

LOCATION: NORTHERN AFRICA

LANGUAGE: ARABIC

POPULATION: 76,117,421

SIZE: 1,001,450 SQ KM

(3 TIMES THE SIZE OF NEW MEXICO)

CAPITAL CITY: CAIRO

FAVE LANDMARKS: **THE PYRAMIDS & THE SPHINX**

FAVE FOOD: SHISH KEBAB

FAVE ANIMAL: CROCODILES

MY FAVE CITIES: ALEXANDRIA & SUEZ

FASHION CAPITAL: CAIRO

FAVE HOBBIES: SNAKE CHARMING &

FINDING ANCIENT TREASURES

FLAG:

MAP:

ALEXANDRIA
PYRAMIDS ★
& SPHINX
SUEZ
CAIRO
EGYPT

28

Ancient **EGYPTIANS** drew all over their walls. Instead of *writing words*, they used these cute little pictures called 'hieroglyphics' (C below) — sort of like MY secret code!

* ANCIENT EGYPTIAN ALPHABET *

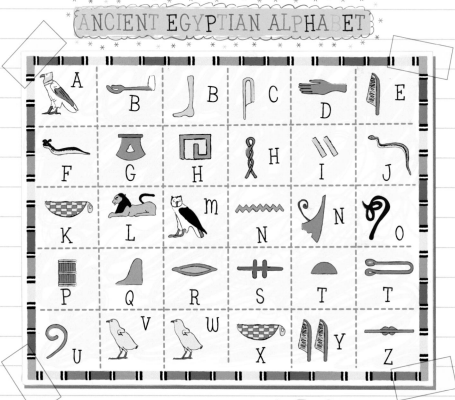

A	B	B
C	D	E
F	G	H	H	I	J
K	L	m	N	N	O
P	Q	R	S	T	T
U	V	W	X	Y	Z

Ancient **EGYPT** was ruled by Kings & Queens (a.k.a. Pharaohs). The most powerful & famous Queen EVER was '**CLEOPATRA**' — a total beauty queen.

Hmmm... *imagine* being CLEOPATRA...?

The perfect life: being pampered & royal!

These R my royal servants...honoring me with my every wish!

WET PAINT

Cleopatra became Queen when she was only 17. She reigned between 51 BC-30 BC & died @ the age of 39.

Niko Popadopolas is next. His *finger* lands on GREECE which is a huge coincidence, considering he's Greek.

GEOGRAPHY
IMAGINE YOU ARE FROM GREECE...?

GREEKS RULE

these R the Olympic Rings — the symbol of the Olympics. They represent the 5 major regions of the world: Africa,

Ms. B said the Olympic Games ⬤⬤⬤ 1st started in GREECE in 776 BC, which was like, AGES ago!

Hmmm... *imagine* ME as an Olympian?!! Actually, better still, *imagine* Fifi-belle! (she's heaps better @ running compared 2 ME.) Hmmm...wonder if they have Doggie Olympics? Fifi-belle would 4 sure win GOLD IN.............

DOGGIE ⬤⬤⬤ OLYMPICS
SILVER   GOLD   BRONZE

this is a traditional Greek 'key' pattern

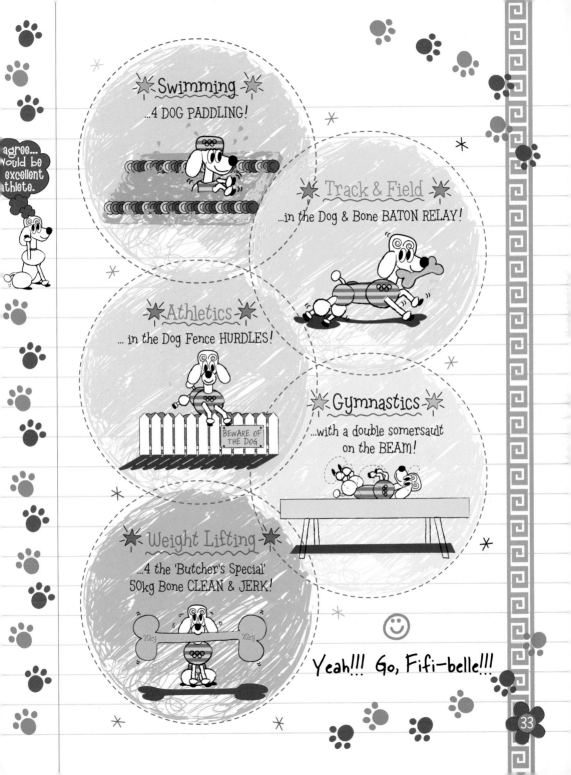

Swimming
...4 DOG PADDLING!

Track & Field
...in the Dog & Bone BATON RELAY!

Athletics
... in the Dog Fence HURDLES!

BEWARE OF THE DOG

Gymnastics
...with a double somersault on the BEAM!

Weight Lifting
...4 the 'Butcher's Special' 50kg Bone CLEAN & JERK!

agree... would be excellent athlete.

Yeah!!! Go, Fifi-belle!!!

Olympic rings

Greek column

olive branch crown

Cats! What about dogs?

ancient Greek vase

GREECE
COOL FACTS & FIGURES

LOCATION: SOUTHERN EUROPE

LANGUAGE: GREEK

POPULATION: 10,647,529

SIZE: 131,940 SQ KM

(SLIGHTLY SMALLER THAN ALABAMA)

CAPITAL CITY: ATHENS

FAVE LANDMARK: THE ACROPOLIS

FAVE FOOD: SOUVLAKI

FAVE ANIMALS: CATS & DONKEYS

MY FAVE CITIES: RHODES, MYKONOS & KOS

FASHION CAPITAL: ATHENS

FAVE HOBBIES:

DANCING & PLATE

SMASHING

MAP:

GREECE

ACROPOLIS

ATHENS

•MYKONOS

KOS•

RHODES

FLAG:

Hmmm...what a champion **Fifi-BELLE** could B!!!!!

Mental note: investigate Doggie Olympics.

Must get Fifi in training. Hmmm...i wonder...

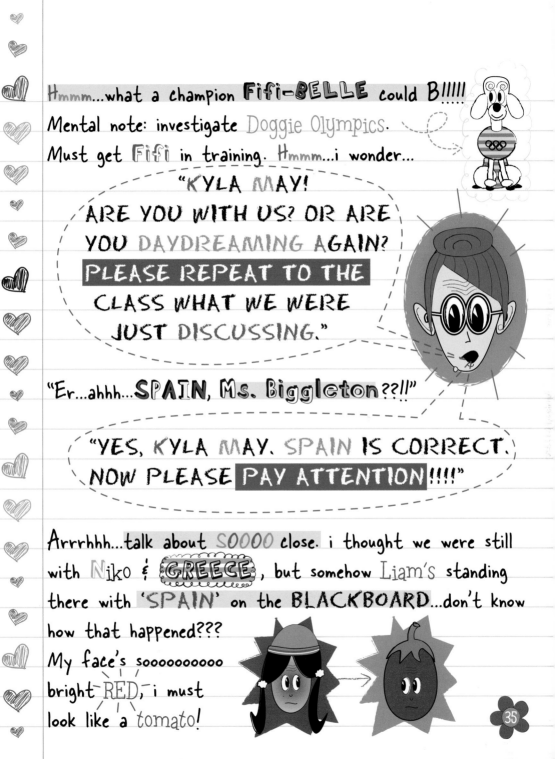

"KYLA MAY! ARE YOU WITH US? OR ARE YOU DAYDREAMING AGAIN? PLEASE REPEAT TO THE CLASS WHAT WE WERE JUST DISCUSSING."

"Er...ahhh...SPAIN, Ms. Biggleton??!!"

"YES, KYLA MAY. SPAIN IS CORRECT. NOW PLEASE PAY ATTENTION!!!!"

Arrrhhh...talk about SOOOO close. i thought we were still with Niko & GREECE, but somehow Liam's standing there with 'SPAIN' on the BLACKBOARD...don't know how that happened???

My face's soooooooooo bright RED, i must look like a tomato!

Oops, **Miki** & Sienna gave me heaps of grief after **clas**
4 getting caught daydreaming. Like, they're T☺TALLY
streSSSSSing out. ☹

Phew...Luckily **class** ended b4 our turn
2 spin. There4 we still have 2night 2 com
up with a country of OUR choice. ☺

Ms. B again stressed the **project** must B
"creative." Surely it can't B this hard. Like,
"creative" is MOST DEFINITELY my thing!

???!?!?

Hmmm...NOW i'm feeling streSSed
...still can't think of ANYTHING??!
...what shall ♡ i do???? ☹

Hmmm...usually when i'm streSSed i
go 2 the beach with **Fifi-BELLE**
2 our 'special secret spot'
@ the end of my street.

Yep...that's what i'll do...come on, **Fifi**...☺

i feel so much better. This place makes me SOOO HaPPY. "Yeah, Good Girl!" Fifi-belle must agree, 'cause her tail's wagging nonstop.

4. GOOD IDEAS WILL COME

3. BREATHE

IMAGINE I'M FROM ------?

2. RELAX

1. CLEAR YOUR MIND

GEOGRAPHY

Good Girl, Fifi-belle
1. Good Girl

Mum says when you're streSSed, U must CLEAR YOUR MIND...RELAX & BREATHE. Good ideas will then come. i think it's called meditation or something. She always does it & calls it "Getting into her Zone."

OK, now my head's clear...let's think...IMAGINE I'M FROM...? Hmmm...mayB Norway?...or Greenland?...what about China? Portugal? New Zealand? Oh, SOOOOO many 2 choose from!

C'mon, KYLA MAY, B CREATIVE!...

Yippeeeee...i've got the BEST iDEA eVER! (Fifi agrees! Her tail's going MANiC!) But i don't want 2 risk writing my iNCREDiBLE, AMAZiNG iDEA in my *journal*, Bianca so want 2 win, bet she'd even sneak a loo[k]

i'm Brilliant (like, of course!)

Just told MUM & DAD my *brilliant idea* & they R soooo impressed. They reckon it's like TOTALLY CREATiVE Wow, my MUM & DAD R the Coolest Parents...well, like 90% of the time (not the 10%, when i'm in trouble).

Yes, my tail reveals my emotions.

PiE GRAPH of MUM & DAD's COOLNESS

10%

Cool Parents NOT!!

90% Cool Parents

Oops! ...in trouble (again!)

NAUGHTY GiRL

Yippeeeee...so can't wait 2 tell the girls 2morrow. CU later!

Oh my Gosh! The weirdest thing just happened......i told Miki & Sienna my brilliant idea...& they were like not totally convinced. (hmmm...i've heard geniuses R often misunderstood!) But then, as we were sort of squabbling over my (unrecognized genius) idea, Bianca came over & like TOTALLY showed off HER so-called "brilliant" project idea...Pleeeease, like her attitude is way out of control. 4 once i didn't know what 2 say!

...& then, 2 my total & utter SURPRISE, Miki blurted out that i also had a brilliant idea, as Sienna put her arm around ME in support! Now the girls LOVVVVE my idea! Talk about my bEstE T fR EndS totally defending me against Bianca. (yeahhh – @ last my genius is recognized!!!)

really 'my'...but since i'm such a team player...'our.'
btw: it's always best 2 B a 'team player.'

We couldn't wait 2 tell Ms. B our idea – who (surprise, surprise) thinks it's BRILLIANT! The girls feel so much better now.

like, of course

But, we'd better get cracking! Only 2 days left! Eeeek! DON'T STRESS, KYLA MAY!...don't stress... breathe...relax...breeeeatheeeeeeeeeeeeee...

Back @ my house we start our research. MUM & DAD teach us about working with *a deadline* – how 2 plan & divide up the workload. (doh! this means i can't g[...] the girls 2 do ALL my work!!!)

MUM & DAD **work** from **home**, so they show us how 2 set up a 'HOME OFFICE.'

Don't ask me what Mum's painting!?!? She's an 'abstract' painter...which means her art doesn't look like anything in particular! But she's a major success & legend in the 'art world' i'd LOVE 2 B a successful artist like Mum one day.

I love helping Kyla May with her homework.

i love 2 work on the floor

BIRDS
Dictio[...]
Flora & Fauna Encyclopedia
Sea life
Native[...]
Encyclopedia A-K
Your Landscape
HISTORY 4 U
Encyclopedia L-Z

i'm totally inquisitive. which means i love 2 research...hmmm...mayB when i grow u[...] ...i'll B a journalist or a detective...those R jobs that require heaps of researching.

Kyla, Miki & Sienna's Home Office
(no daydreaming allowed)

this is what Mum & Dad helped us organize

Geography Project
To do:

♥ Kyla ♥	♥ Miki ♥	♥ Sienna ♥
✓ research books & encyclopedias	✓ research on internet	✓ research on internet
☐ write up info	✓ go to library	☐ photocopy info
✓ don't daydream	☐ list main topics	☐ list main topics
☐ find pictures	☐ write presentation script	☐ write presentation script
☐ list main topics	✓ make sure Kyla doesn't daydream	✓ make sure Kyla doesn't daydream
☐ think of presentation ideas	☐ help Kyla with presentation rehearsal	☐ type up presentation script
☐ rehearse presentation		✓ make hot chocolates
☐ don't daydream		

usually of course it's really Mum & Dad's home office, or as they call it – their 'Studio'

Geography Project Deadline
DAYS LEFT: Presentation day

WED	THUR	FRI

2 days 2 do everything!! Eeek!

this was our 'brainstorming'

agriculture
resources
industry
technology
indigenous
history
culture
city life vs. country life
wildlife

Imagine you are

from _____ ?

Population
religion
ethnic groups
standard of living
climate

landmarks
discovery
natives
wonders of the world
art

Dad always oversees us when we use the internet

guess which chair is usually Mum's & which is Dad's? (pretty obvious really)

41

SORRY!!! Apologies 4 not writing 4 ages — but i've been totally busy with *our amazing, brilliant* **project**. We've worked SOOOO hard & we're full-on EXHAUSTED

The girls decided i'm the most 'theatrical', there4 i'm presenting 2 the **class** 2morrow...but, i'm not nervous @ all 'cause U know how much i LVVVVVVVE performing in front of an audience!!! i'm a NATURAL (so everyone says)

FINISH LINE

YUM

YUM!!!

YUM, save some for me!

Yippee   COOL   Yeahhhhhhhh!

1 million

YUM x 1,000,000 — **Mum**'s made **Chocolate Chip Cookies** 2 celebrate finishing our **project**. Ohhhhhhhhhhhhhh, they R ABSOLUTELY INCREDILICIOUS!!

(incredible + delicious)

Hey...here's Mum's recipe

Chocolate Chip Cookies

2 ¼ cups all-purpose flour
1 teaspoon baking soda
1 teaspoon salt
1 cup (2 sticks, ½ pound) butter, softened
¾ cup granulated (white) sugar
¾ cup packed brown sugar
1 teaspoon vanilla extract
2 eggs
2 cups (12-ounce package) Semisweet Chocolate Chips

- -

Combine flour, baking soda & salt in small bowl. Beat butter, granulated sugar, brown sugar & vanilla in large mixer bowl. Add eggs 1 at a time, beating well after each addition; gradually beat in flour mixture. Stir in chips. Drop rounded tablespoons of mixture onto ungreased baking sheets.

Bake in preheated 375-degree (Fahrenheit) oven for 9-11 minutes or until golden brown. Let stand for 2 minutes; remove to wire racks until completely cool.

Only bake with your Mum or another adult!

i feel SO excited & now a little nervous about our presentation 2morrow...better get some sleep...
Good Night. xxx

It's GEOGRAPHY class & i'm starting 2 feel EXTREMELY nervous – i' even got **butterflies** in my tummy!

...When i was little, i T☺TALLY believed real-life **butterflies** lived inside my tummy!

Yes, we get "butterflies" but we call them "fleas."

Hmmm...i wonder if dogs get **butterflies** 2? Hmmm...

Hmmm...

Hmmm...

Oops...CONCENTRATE, KYLA MAY!!!

...STOP GeTTiNG DISTRaCtED!...

Hey...Mr. Boticelli (Bianca's dad) has just come in2 **class**

Hmmm...what's he doing here ?????????????????????????????

Tara Tiara goes **1st** with her group's presentation on **America**.

Gosh, talk about boooooring (Zzzzzzzzzzzz). Like, i've been 2 America & it's TOTALLY the most exciting place EVER. Can't believe her group didn't get that!

♥ But Tara's presentation was riveting in comparison 2 Amber Van Wiggle's, who went 2nd with EGYPT...

Zzz Zzzzzz Zzzzzz Zzzzzz Zzzzzz Zzzzzz Zzzzzz Z
zzzzzz Zzzzzz Zzzzzz Zzzzzz Zzzzzz Zzzzzz Zzz

i think Wally has actually fallen asleep! (Hee hee, how much does he look like a monkey now!)

Hello!!! Amber didn't even mention CLEOPATRA or the Sphinx or hieroglyphics...like full-on B☹☹☹RING.........

Zzzzzz Zzzzzz Zzzzzz Zzzzzz Zzzzzz Zzzzzz Zzz
zzz Zzzzzz Zzzzzz Zzzzzz Zzzzzz Zzzzzz Zzzzzz Z

♡ ...Oh no, i'm starting 2 nod off...WAKE UP, KYLA ...must focus...must not daydream...what shall i do??...i can't get in TROUBLE...i know—i'll write lines 2 stay focused!!!!

I must always concentrate in class
I must always concentrate in class
I must always concentrate in class
I must always concentrate in class
I must always concentrate in class
I must always concentrate in class
I must always concentrate in class
I must always concentrate in class
I must always concentrate in class
I must always concentrate in class
I must always concentrate in class
I must always concentrate in class
I must always concentrate in class
I must always concentrate in class

☺ Thank goodness, it's time 4 the next **group!!!** Niko's up presenting ‖ANCIENT‖GREECE‖ (...that's V. creative, instead of Greece 2day, he's doing ‖GREECE‖ thousands of years ago.)

Did U know Ancient Greeks honored Gods & Goddesses?! 4 sure, my FAVE Gods R: **ZEUS**, who was the BIG boss of all Gods, God of heaven & earth...

Zeus's weapon is a thunder-bolt so U don't want 2 get him angry!

ZEUS

Poseidon's weapon is a trident, which can "shake the earth." Scary!

POSEIDON

The Gods live in Heaven, of course

xcuse me!
I am the
Goddess
of Love,
Desire
& Beauty!!!

Also **POSEIDON**, Lord of the Sea. ♥ My absolute no. 1 FAVE **Goddess** ever is ♥ 🡒 **Aphrodite**, Goddess of L♥vE, Desire & Beauty.

Aphrodite

Aphrodite has the power 2 make anyone she wants love her. Cool...wish i could do that.

These R Ancient Greek IONIC columns. used 2 hold up buildings.

Hmmm...i'd love 2 B an ANCIENT GREEK Goddess...how about the Goddess of...

...hmmm...hmmm...

Hey...& Fifi-belle could B the **Goddess** of **French Poodles** (like, of course!) ☺

CYLA MAY

HEALTH SPA

BEAUTY SALON

Olive branch crowns R symbols of peace & unity.

The olive tree is a symbol of Greek culture, freedom & peace. It's Greece's most precious tree.

Ancient Greek vases R some of the World's most treasured pieces of art.

49

Ouchhhhhh!!!!! (Miki) just pinched me! (But like i s'pose it TOTALLY understandable, 'cause i was completely lost my (imagination) as "KYLA MAY, Goddess BEAUTY SALONS & HEALTH SPAS.")

Finally it's Bianca's turn, (eek, we're next – my **butterflies** R going craaaaaaaaaaaaaaaaaazy).

Bianca's presenting her team's project on **Italy**. Just lo @ her, so smug as she walks 2 the front!

...What??? i can't believe it!!!! Bianca just said her dad's here 2 "help with the sophisticated aspects of her presentation"...PLEASE, like surely that's so NOT allowed. She can't possibly B serious, can she??????????

Perfect Bianca Boticelli

smug as a bug

BuuZZZz ZzzZZZz

the Italian flag

My fave Italian food is Pizza & Spaghetti Bolognese, oh, & Linguine Marinara & Gelati & Tiramisu, also Lasagne..Mmmm...so yummy!

ohhh, so cute!

this is Italian 4 'beautiful'

Italy is 4 sure the most 'bellissimo' country ever. i don't know which city i adore more: Rome? Florence? Venice? Milan? Naples? Every city is totally 'fantastico'!

this is Italian 4 'fantastic'

Italy is really, really OLD & famous 4 its *ancient* buildings, incredible *art*, *fashion* & delicious FOOD.

this is Italian 4 'Mum & Dad'

(Now i feel hungry!)

My 'Mama & Papa' actually "fell in love" there ages ago. They met @ the 'Colosseum' in Rome (**Italy**'s capital city), while having Gelati (yummy Italian ice cream). How cuuuuuuute! Here's a pic of the magical moment:

Mum looks like an Italian Movie star. Dad looks exactly the same. They noticed each other 'cause they had the same flavor gelati.

1 day i so want 2 go 2 Italy — mayB i will "fall in love" there 2?! But like NOT till i'm a grown-up of course.

The Colosseum is the most famous monument of Rome. It was built in 75-80 AD & was a stadium 4 concerts, plays, chariot races & gladiator fights. It held 45,000 people!

51

♥ i must admit Bianca's presentation on **Italy** is awesome, but it's soooo obvious Mr. Boticelli prepared the entire thing!!! Like, as if an 11-year-old could create a presentation like this? No way, José!

Surely Bianca will get in2 full-on TROUBLE 4 this — hah, what a once in a lifetime moment!
(If only **Fifi-belle** were here 2 share in this special event!)

You can tell me about it ...over & over again!

That's my girl!

Mr. Boticelli

laptop computer

laser pointer

remote mouse

projector connected 2 laptop computer

Venice's famous gondolas

Spaghetti Bolognese

Tuscan houses R gorgeous

Soccer is the fave sport of Italy

MILAN

the Leaning Tower of Pisa

54

Italian shoes R the best

the home of café latte

gelato

pizza delicious

ROME

ITALY
COOL FACTS & FIGURES

LOCATION: SOUTHERN EUROPE

LANGUAGE: ITALIAN

POPULATION: 58,057,477

SIZE: 301,230 SQ KM

(SLIGHTLY LARGER THAN ARIZONA)

CAPITAL CITY: ROME

FAVE LANDMARK: LEANING TOWER OF PISA

FAVE FOOD: SPAGHETTI BOLOGNESE

FAVE ANIMAL: SQUID

MY FAVE CITIES: MILAN, FLORENCE & VENICE

FASHION CAPITAL: MILAN

FAVE HOBBIES:

SHOPPING, EATING &

MORE SHOPPING

MILAN
PISA
VENICE
LEANING TOWER OF PISA
FLORENCE
ROME
MAP:
ITALY

FLAG:

★☆★☆★☆★☆★★☆�★☆★☆★★☆★☆★☆★★☆★☆★☆

^ Time 4 our presentation. ✿ ♡ ✿

★☆★☆★☆★☆★★☆★☆★☆★★☆★☆★☆★★☆★☆★☆

Good Luck!

♡ i walk up 2 the front of the **class** & stand there. Just ME ...NO photos, NO papier-mâché models, NO posters, NO gizmos — NOTHING! (See, Bianca!)

⭐ Everyone's totally confused — whispering, worried something's gone wrong. They think i've forgotten our presentation! i bet they think i'm going 2 get in trouble!

⭐ i clear my throat & the chattering stops — i get everyone's undivided attention before i begin.

⭐ i ask the **class** 2 close their eyes & clear their minds.

"close your eyes..."

"clear your minds..."

⭐ The **class** looks @ one another like T☺TALLY confused, but do as they R told.

i then say in a V. calm voice:
"i'd like U all 2 *imagine* that YOU'RE a tropical fish, swimming in the most amazing reef in the world. U R surrounded by vibrant coral in all the colors of the rainbow. *Imagine* your happiness as U explore YOUR endless tropical paradise. On YOUR travels U C a beautiful shell that reflects all the shades of the ocean.

Yes...
I'm imagining...

"...Now *imagine* YOU'RE that shell, tossing & turning in the warm ocean water. U wash up on the most spectacular beach ever. This beach is **heaven** on **earth**. A little girl picks U up; she *giggles* as she runs along the soft white sand."

Go, Kyla!

"...Now *imagine* YOU'RE the little girl, playing with YOUR family & friends, collecting shells & making sandcastles. U C a shadow on the sand & look up 2 C the most incredible eagle soaring across the vast deep blue sky...

...still imagining...

"...*Imagine* YOU'RE that eagle, gliding with grace over breath-taking snow-capped mountains. As U soar higher & higher...

"Eventually U reach a sunburned land, covered with red rock formations & Aboriginal history. As U soar, U C a kangaroo basking in the late afternoon sun.

"...Now imagine YOU'RE that kangaroo. The sun is setting as U travel over the amazing land that is YOUR home."

Yay! everyone's totally in2 it!

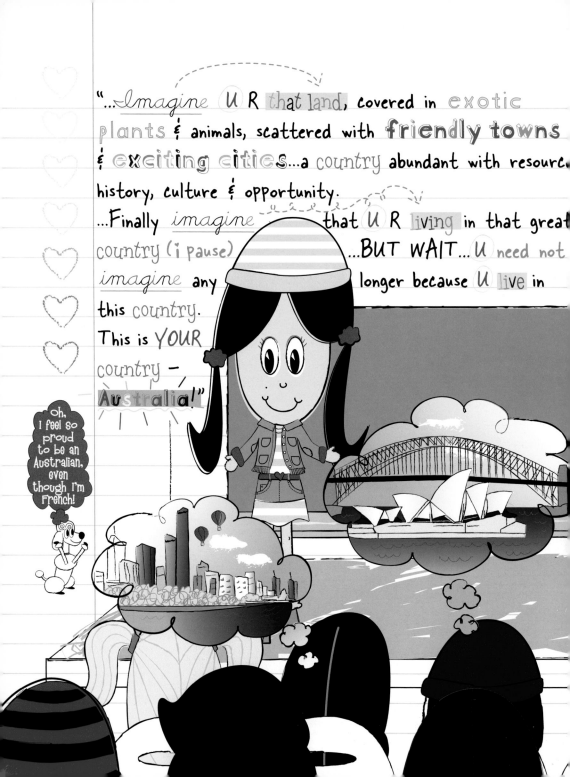

Uluru: world's largest monolith & sacred Aboriginal site

Sydney Opera House

tree leaves

WOMBAT— o CUTE!!!

clown fish
Queensland's
Great Barrier
Reef

grass tree: so funny looking!

AUSTRALIA
COOL FACTS & FIGURES

LOCATION: BETWEEN INDIAN & SOUTH PACIFIC OCEAN

LANGUAGE: ENGLISH, NATIVE LANGUAGES

POPULATION: 19,913,144

SIZE: 7,686,850 SQ KM
(SLIGHTLY SMALLER THAN THE U.S.)

CAPITAL CITY: CANBERRA

FAVE LANDMARKS: ULURU & GREAT BARRIER REEF

FAVE FOOD: SEAFOOD & BBQ

FAVE ANIMALS: KOALAS, WOMBATS & KANGAROOS

MY FAVE CITIES: MELBOURNE, SYDNEY & PERTH

FASHION CAPITAL: MELBOURNE

FAVE HOBBIES: SURFING & SWIMMING

FLAG:

MAP:

GREAT BARRIER REEF★

ULURU ★
AUSTRALIA

PERTH
CANBERRA
SYDNEY
MELBOURNE

KOALA— Totally CUTE!!! (don't U reckon my name sounds a little like 'koala'? This was my nickname when i was younger.)

shells from beautiful Aussie beaches

Rialto Towers, Melbourne — where i come from!!!

Yeah! The entire **class** was SOOO totally mesmeriz

As they came back 2 reality, they clapped & cheered

nonstop. That was UNREAL!!! i got the entire **class** 2

C Australia thru the eyes of a visitor.

C, i 1st got the idea @ my 'special secret spot

with Fifi-BELLE, when i overheard a girl with an

'American' accent say how beautiful the beach was

how C☺☺L it would B 2 live here. i realized then how

lucky i was 2 have MY beach. i also realized that we

often 4get 2 B thankful 4 our surroundings...appreciat

our OWN world - our OWN country. MUM says U must

"always appreciate your own backyard." Time & agai

we TAKE what WE HAVE 4 GRANTED.

There4, why not "imagine coming from Australia"?

Our presentation reminded the **class** of how fantabulou

our country is & how lucky WE R 2 B Australian.

But the bEstE T thing of all was everyone T☺TALLY

experienced MY world, a world of living thru your

imagination. YIPPEEEEEE! (how brilliant!)

U must agree...it was a brilliant idea. i am no doubt a TOTAL genius...if i say so myself!!!

Ms. B awarded our group TOP MARKS 'cause we not only used OUR *imagination*, but we also got the class 2 use THEIR *imagination*! YEAHHHHH! i'm soooooooo happy!

Miki, Sienna & i can't stop jumping up & down. (so can't wait 2 tell **Fifi-belle**, **Mum** & **Dad**! They will B extremely proud 'cause i used my *imagination* ...& didn't get in2 TROUBLE!)

bestest friends 4 ever

Ahhh...U'll never guess what? Ms. B wants Bianca & her Dad 2 stay behind! Ms. B doesn't look V. happy. U don't need an *imagination* 2 guess what will happen next!?!!!!

Hmmm...mayB GEOGRAPHY class isn't so B☹☹☹RING after all! Catch ya next time. ☺

KYLA MAY's Dictionary:

2	=	to/too
2day	=	today
2morrow	=	tomorrow
2nite	=	tonight
4	=	for
4get	=	forget
B	=	be
B4	=	before
btw.	=	by the way
C	=	see
fantabulous	=	fantastic + fabulous
in2	=	into
incredilicious	=	incredible + delicious
mayB	=	maybe
R	=	are
there4	=	therefore
U	=	you
V.	=	very
@	=	at
&	=	and
=	=	equals

i give U permission 2 use my dictionary with your friends!